P9-CDC-572

THE TRAIL ON WHICH THEY WEPT

The Story of a Cherokee Girl

Sarah Tsaluh Rogers

THE TRAIL ON WHICH THEY WEPT

The Story of a Cherokee Girl

BY DOROTHY AND THOMAS HOOBLER

AND CAREY-GREENBERG ASSOCIATES

PICTURES BY S. S. BURRUS

SILVER BURDETT PRESS

Copyright © 1992 by
Carey-Greenberg Associates
Illustrations © 1992 by S.S. Burrus

All rights reserved including the
right of reproduction in
whole or in part in any form.
Published by Silver Burdett Press, Inc.,
a division of Simon & Schuster, Inc.,
250 James Street
Morristown, NJ 07960
Designed by Leslie Bauman

Illustrations on pages 54, 56 and 57
by Leslie Dunlap

Manufactured in the
United States of America

10 9 8 7 6 5 4

Library of Congress Cataloging-in-Publication Data

Hoobler, Dorothy.
The trail on which they wept :
the story of a Cherokee girl /
by Dorothy and Thomas Hoobler
and Carey-Greenberg Associates ;
pictures by S.S. Burrows.
p.   cm.—(Her story)
Summary: Forced to leave their homes in Georgia
in 1837, Sarah Tsaluh Rogers, her family, and other
Cherokees make the long and difficult journey along the
Trail of Tears to the Indian Territory in Oklahoma.
1. Cherokee Removal, 1838—Juvenile fiction.
[1. Cherokee Removal, 1838—Fiction.   2. Cherokee
Indians—History—Fiction.   3. Indians of North
America—Southern States—History—Fiction.
4. Family life—Fiction.]   I. Hoobler, Thomas.
II. Burrows, S. S., ill.   III. Carey-Greenberg
Associates.   IV. Title.   V. Series.
PZ7.H76227Tq   1992
[Fic]—dc20   91-34465 CIP AC
ISBN 0-382-24353-6 (pbk.) ISBN 0-382-24331-5 (lib. bdg.)

Curr
PZ
7
.H 76227
Tq
1992

CONTENTS

CHAPTER ONE

This Land Is Ours!

IT WAS harvest time in the land of the Cherokees. At dawn, from the front porch of her family's house, Sarah Tsaluh Rogers watched blue mist rise above the floor of the valley. She stepped onto the grass, feeling the dew tickle her bare feet. The rising sun gradually lit up the hills in the distance. Every tree was ablaze with gold and crimson leaves.

It was a wonderful sight, but in the back of Sarah's mind was the thought: Will this be the last harvest?

The year had been a good one on the Rogers plantation. The workers had filled wagon after wagon with corn, taking it to the mill to be ground into meal. The corn plants had been gathered into sheaves and left to dry.

The hard work of picking the cotton was finally finished. The plantation had produced nearly a thousand bales, and Sarah's family had sold them for a high price. When the trees lost the last of their leaves and winter came, the big plantation house would be warm, and there would be more than enough food for everyone.

But then the sun went behind a cloud. A chilly breeze blew down from the hills. Sarah wrapped her arms around her body, thinking again of the shadow that hung over her people.

The state government of Georgia wanted the Cherokees to leave their land. For years the Cherokees had fought Georgia in the courts. Finally the Supreme Court of the United States had ruled in favor of the Cherokees.

But President Andrew Jackson would not enforce the Supreme Court's order. He wanted the Cherokees to move hundreds of miles west, across the Mississippi River. He said they would be happier there. Of course everyone knew that wasn't true. The Cherokees were happy right here in the land where they had always lived.

It's our land! Sarah thought angrily. We won't leave it!

Many Cherokees felt the same way. Although some had moved west, others refused to go. And, now, perhaps they had reason to hope.

For at the beginning of that year, 1837, President Jackson has retired. The United States had a new president, Martin Van Buren. John Ross, the chief that the Cherokees had elected, had gone to Washington, D.C., to meet President Van Buren. Ross would ask the new president to let the Cherokees stay on their land.

Ross had left two months ago. Sarah and her family, and all the rest of the Cherokees, waited for him to return and tell them what had happened. But so far, they had no word.

Sarah's head buzzed with thoughts and questions. She decided to walk into the hills and visit her grandmother.

Grandmother lived alone in the log lodge that she and her husband had built. Although Grandfather had been a white trapper, the Cherokees had welcomed him. When he and grandmother married, he became a Cherokee too.

That was the Cherokee way. Cherokees also had welcomed Christian missionaries to their land. Over the years, many Cherokees had become Christians, like Sarah's family. That was why so many of them had white names.

But not Grandmother, even though she had married a white man. She was a *ghighau,* a respected old woman who kept the Cherokee traditions alive. When her son, Sarah's father, had built the big plantation house, he asked her to come and live there. But Grandmother refused. "Too much like a *unaka* house," she said. Like the other old people, Grandmother called the whites *unakas.*

Sarah could smell Grandmother's cooking pot even before she came to the lodge. Grandmother looked up as she stirred the pot over the fire. "Tsaluh," she said. "What have you come to ask me?"

Grandmother always called Sarah by her Cherokee name. And she knew that her grandchild Tsaluh always visited when she had questions.

"What are you cooking today, Grandmother?" Tsaluh asked with a smile.

"Squirrel stew," Grandmother replied. "Nice fat squirrel, full of acorns. But to make it taste good, you have to find other things. Onions, chestnuts, good-tasting roots—I told you this before. Has that Christian schoolteacher made you forget all the Cherokee ways?"

"No, Grandmother."

"So what did you come to ask me? Has John Ross come back yet?"

Even Grandmother wanted to know, Tsaluh thought. She shook her head. "Not yet. But, Grandmother, what will we do if he says we have to move?"

Grandmother snorted. "Do? We'll act like Cherokees. Who gave us this land, Tsaluh?"

"The Great Spirit," Tsaluh said, because she knew the answer Grandmother wanted.

"Right! Not the Americans. Not George Washington, though he said we could stay here too. We let them write it down on a paper, because the *unakas* worship paper. But that was a mistake."

Grandmother motioned for Tsaluh to come closer. She took a piece of yarn and wrapped it around her granddaughter's waist. "You're almost a woman," she muttered. "Time I made a medicine belt for you. Then I'll show you how to gather herbs for it."

Tsaluh was pleased. But she had another question. "Why was it a mistake, Grandmother?" she asked.

"Mm? Oh, the paper. Yes. Because the words on the paper were in the *unaka* language. Later on, the *unakas* said the Cherokees did not understand. The paper did not mean what we thought. That was when Sequoyah had his big idea."

Grandmother tapped the side of her head. "People thought Sequoyah was touched by an evil spirit. He stayed all the time in his house and made marks on bark."

She chuckled. "His wife was very angry with him because he never cared about anything but those marks. But at last he figured out how to write the Cherokee language. And from then on, nobody could fool us. Because we had our own writing."

Tsaluh nodded. "I know how to read and write both Cherokee and English. We use the Cherokee newspaper in school."

"Good girl. But what do they call you in that school?"

Tsaluh looked down. "The teacher calls me Sarah."

"See there? *Unaka* name." Grandmother spat out the word.

"I have both names," Tsaluh said. "Mother and Father chose them for me."

Grandmother shook her head. "No, no. I chose Tsaluh for you when you were born. I held you in my arms, my first girl grandchild, and I called you Tsaluh."

"I never knew that before," Tsaluh said.

"I saw you were a real Cherokee," Grandmother said. "Like me. Like Sequoyah himself. You are like him. You have the gift to see things that have not yet been and make them come true."

Grandmother reached out and took Tsaluh's hand. "But if you don't want to lose that gift, you must always be Tsaluh. Sarah can never have that gift, for she is *unaka*. Tsaluh is Cherokee."

Sarah thought about this. She watched Grandmother tie the ends of the yarn that she would make into a belt. Grandmother's fingers were bent and wrinkled, but she worked quickly, hardly looking at the yarn.

"Grandmother?" Tsaluh said. "Is it true that Sequoyah has gone to the western land where Andrew Jackson wants the Cherokees to go?"

Grandmother's hands stopped, and she glanced at Tsaluh. "That's true," she said. "He wanted to see what the land is like. He is a wanderer. But he knows where his home is. He is old now, like me. When the Raven Mockers come for him, he will return."

Tsaluh shivered. The Raven Mockers were the

spirits that came after your soul when you died. If you didn't have someone to watch you die, the Raven Mockers would take it.

"He'll come back," Grandmother said firmly. "And we must be here to send his soul back to the stars where the first Cherokees came from. If Sequoyah dies in the west, in the Darkening Land, the Raven Mockers will take his soul."

In school Sarah had learned that the sun really doesn't sink into the Darkening Land at night. It vanishes because the Earth turns. But she had never seen that for herself. Tsaluh, the Cherokee part of her, still believed that maybe the sun really went west to the Darkening Land each day and died. Who was right? Sarah? Or Tsaluh?

The sound of hoofbeats broke into her thoughts. She ran and looked down the path. It was Sam, her younger brother, looking as if he were fleeing from the Raven Mockers himself.

"Sarah!" he called, reining in the horse. "Father sent me to find you. Is Grandmother here?"

"Of course she is. What's the matter?"

"Some people from Georgia have come, and they brought soldiers. They want us to get out of our house! They say they own it now!"

CHAPTER TWO

We Must Save the Children

SARAH rode back on the horse with Sam. Grandmother wouldn't come with them. She said she wasn't afraid, because even the *unakas* wouldn't bother an old woman.

When they arrived home, they saw a crowd of people in front of the house. Some of their neighbors had arrived carrying hoes and hatchets. The soldiers were looking around nervously, for even though they had guns, there were only five of them.

Father was standing on the front porch, arguing with a big man with a red face. Both of them were shouting. Another soldier, wearing a sword at his belt, kept trying to push them apart.

The big man kept saying, "I won it. Fair and square." He was waving a paper at Father.

Mother stepped out of the crowd when Sarah and Sam came up. She said, "Can you imagine? He says he won our land in a lottery."

"That's not fair!" Sarah said. "How could anyone think that was right?"

Mother shook her head. "I don't know, Sarah," she said. "I don't know what will happen."

The soldier on the porch held up his hands and faced the crowd. "There's no need for trouble," he shouted. "Everybody, listen to me. My orders are to carry out the relocation peacefully."

An angry murmur passed through the crowd. *Relocation*—that was the word Andrew Jackson had used to describe his plan to move the Cherokees. Sarah hated the sound of it, and so did everyone else.

Father took the soldier's arm and said, "When John Ross gets back, he'll tell you to change your orders."

The crowd cheered. "John Ross!" some of the people yelled. "Wait for Chief John Ross!"

"He's come back," the soldier shouted at them. "And he'll tell you all what you have to do." A silence followed. People in the crowd looked at each other. Could it be true?

The soldier turned to the big man who said he had won the Rogers' land. "As for you, it won't hurt to wait a couple of days to let these people prepare to leave. Get back in your carriage and follow us."

The man protested, but Sarah could see he was too afraid to stay without the soldiers. He did as he was told. The crowd moved aside to let him pass.

Before the soldiers rode off, Sarah's father spoke a few more words with them. "They say John Ross will be at the town of Red Clay this evening," Father told his neighbors. "If he is, we'll hear what he has to say."

He motioned to Sarah and Sam, and they followed him and Mother into the house. Father sat down in a chair. He looked worried. "I fear that what the soldiers say may be true."

"But John Ross couldn't agree to leave," Sarah said. "He's always told us not to give up hope."

Father shook his head. "We'll see. We'll see."

For the rest of the day, Sarah's family acted as if someone had died. Mother walked through the rooms, looking at the furniture, the pictures on the walls, the vases of flowers that she always kept full from her garden. She touched each object as if she knew she would soon be leaving it behind.

We can't just give up like this, Sarah thought. Somebody has got to do something. "Should I tell Grandmother?" she asked Father.

He shook his head. "I'd better go see her myself. Maybe she'll come with us to hear John Ross. I know this will be very hard on her."

Late in the afternoon he returned, bringing Grandmother with him. She was sitting in the buggy when the rest of the family came out. Sarah sat next to her and reached for Grandmother's hand. But she just shook her head. She was still working on the medicine belt. Father snapped the reins, and they headed for Red Clay.

The town had once been a busy place, especially on Saturdays when most people came to shop. All the stores had been owned by Cherokees. But now many had boards nailed over the windows. Their owners had accepted cash payments from the state of Georgia and moved west.

Tonight, Red Clay came alive one last time. Carriages and wagons were arriving from all over the countryside. The people in them wore their best clothes, as if they were coming to church. They wore woolen suits and cotton dresses, and looked very much like people in Boston, Philadelphia, or anywhere else in the United States. But there was one difference. They were Cherokees.

"Look at them," Grandmother said, loudly enough so that others turned their heads. "They wanted to be like the *unakas*. But a Cherokee can't ever be an *unaka*. An *unaka* can become a Cherokee, but not the other way around. It will always be that way."

They helped her out of the buggy and went inside. Sarah and Sam went up to the balcony where the rest of the children were. They looked down and saw Grandmother seated in front with the other old people. The room was already so crowded that people were standing in the back and along the walls.

The crowd hushed, and John Ross stood up. He was a short man, but when he spoke his voice was deep and powerful. "I am sorry it has taken me so long to return," he said. "When the other chiefs and I arrived in Washington, the President would not see us. He sent others to talk in his place. But I said I was the chief of the Cherokee Nation. I would speak only with the chief of the United States."

Sarah saw people's heads nodding in approval. They had voted for John Ross as chief because of his great dignity. He was as great a man as the President of the United States, and they knew it.

"Finally," John Ross continued, "President Van Buren invited me to the White House—alone. He would not let the other chiefs come, though many of his own assistants were there. Perhaps," he said with a smile, "he was afraid of me."

John Ross tapped his chest. "I was not afraid of him." Laughter rang out, but it was a nervous sound. What did the President say? Sarah thought.

"Van Buren told me he was a generous man. He knew that George Washington had promised we could live here forever. But Van Buren said that other Cherokees had agreed to move west."

The crowd murmured in anger. It was true that some Cherokees had taken money for their land. But most had refused. Grandmother had said, "They will spend the money, and soon it will be gone. But land cannot be spent or sold. It is the gift of the Great Spirit."

Ross raised his hand. "Van Buren made me an offer. He said he would pay five million dollars if all the Cherokees would move west."

Sarah's head spun. Five million dollars? How much was that? Father said that all the cotton they had grown that year sold for seven hundred dollars. And he thought that was a lot.

"Five million dollars," Ross said again. "But I had to agree right away. He would not let me come back and ask the people to decide. So I ask you now: What should I have said?"

A moment passed. Then one of the old men near Grandmother shouted, "No!" And the rest of the hall took it up. "No! No!" they all shouted.

Ross nodded, and waved for quiet. "I told Van Buren no. I asked what price he would take for the city of Washington. How much money would he take for the graves of his parents and the house where he was born?" People clapped and shouted.

"But he wouldn't listen," said Ross. "The President has hardened his heart against us."

"Fight him!" shouted an old woman. Sarah could not tell if it was Grandmother. "Yes!" other voices agreed. "We will fight."

But Ross shook his head, and Sarah felt her heart drop. She knew what he was about to say.

"The soldiers are already here. They have guns, and we do not. They are many, and we are few. Let me tell you what they have already done to clear one of our towns. They rounded up all the children and put them into camps. Their parents had to follow, or they would never see their children again."

Angry shouts echoed through the hall. "They won't do that here!" someone said.

"They will do that, and worse," said John Ross. "Van Buren has given the order to drive us out. They will stop at nothing." He looked up to the balcony and pointed right at Sarah. Her spine tingled.

"Our children are our future," said John Ross. "We cannot risk their lives. We cannot keep the Americans from taking our land. We must find another."

People began to weep and shout. John Ross hung his head and listened to all they had to say. But he would not change his decision. Sarah's eyes filled with tears. All she could think was, It isn't right. It isn't right.

CHAPTER THREE

A Dream

THE NEXT few days were a blur of activity to Sarah. Each family could take only what they could carry. Sarah's family was lucky—they had enough horses to pull two wagons. But even so, they would have to leave a lot behind.

Mother gave Sarah a box and told her to fill it with clothes for the journey. The box seemed to grow smaller as Sarah tried to make her choices. She picked out her best dress, a pink organdy frock decorated with little ribbons. She had worn it only once, when her parents had given a big party last year.

Sarah folded the dress carefully, but it still took up more than half the space in the box. The petticoat that Sarah had worn under the dress was almost as large. Sarah added a straw hat that she wore when the sun was hot.

The box was nearly full. Sarah added some other underthings and an extra blouse. Around the plantation, she nearly always went barefoot, but she thought she might need a pair of shoes. After they went in, there was no room for anything else.

When Mother came to look at the box, she shook her head. She sat down with Sarah on the bed. "Dear, I know you don't quite understand what is happening," Mother said.

"I do understand," Sarah said. "But I don't think it's fair."

Mother sighed. "It isn't fair," she said. "But we have to make the best of it. It's going to be colder in the new land than it is here. And there won't be any parties. We're going to have to do a lot of work. We must start a new life." Mother turned her head away, and Sarah realized she was crying.

Sarah hugged her mother. "I'm sorry," she said. She wasn't sure just what she had done wrong, but she didn't want Mother to cry.

Mother emptied the box. "Take the shoes," she said. "And your coat."

"I almost never wear my coat," Sarah said.

"You will need it where we're going," Mother insisted. "And take your plain dresses that you wear in the fields. Anything that will last a long time."

Sarah did what she was told. But when Mother was gone, she tried on the party dress one last time. She looked in the mirror. Would she ever have a pretty dress like this one again? She closed her eyes and tried to see the future, like Grandmother said she could.

But nothing happened. It is because of the dress, she thought. This is Sarah's dress. Sarah, the *unaka*. When I take this dress off, I will be Tsaluh, true Cherokee.

She put on a red dress that Grandmother had made for her. Grandmother had picked sumac berries to make dye to color the cloth. Tsaluh looked at herself in the mirror. She unpinned her hair and let it hang down around her shoulders. This is my future, she thought.

Tsaluh crumpled the party dress and tossed it onto the floor. I will forget it, she thought. I will begin my new life now, like Mother said.

On the last night before they left, Tsaluh walked through the house. Now she understood why Mother had been so sad. She saw everything they had to leave behind. The thing that Mother loved best sat in the parlor—their piano, which Father had brought all the way from Baltimore as a wedding present for Mother.

Mother had taught Sarah how to play it. Sarah looked through the sheet music inside the piano bench. She picked out her favorite song and began to play.

It was "Home, Sweet Home." The song had been written by an *unaka* who was a good friend of the Cherokees. Its music had always made Tsaluh feel warm and safe. But tonight, the sadness she felt made its way through her hands onto the keys.

She felt someone behind her. It was Mother. She put her arms around Tsaluh. "I will always remember that," she said.

"Please, Mother, will you play it?" Tsaluh said.

Mother shook her head. "It's time to sleep now. We must start early tomorrow."

Tsaluh went upstairs and tried to sleep. But the house was full of memories, and they crowded into her head. Racing her brother up and down the big staircase. The times when neighbors came for dinner. It was a Cherokee tradition to welcome visitors with the best food they had to offer. There were always so many people in the house. And they would gather in the parlor while Mother played the piano.

Tsaluh could hear it now. She lifted her head. It *was* Mother. She had decided to play after all, and listening to the music, Tsaluh was able to sleep.

She began to dream. She saw Grandmother, who pointed into the distance. Wagons were moving along, a long line of them, through a strange country Tsaluh had never seen.

The wagons came to a great river. On the other side, night had fallen. No moon shone there, and Tsaluh could not see what the other side was like. It was the Dark Land.

Tsaluh flew into the air. She did not think this strange, for it was a dream. She tried to see across the river, to see what the future would be.

She looked down. On the bank of the river, two girls were fighting. They held each other, rolling across the ground. One of them wore a red dress, and the other a pink dress. Tsaluh . . . and Sarah.

"Stop it!" someone shouted.

She sat up in bed. She was the one who had shouted. She had woken herself up. A sliver of light shone through the curtains at her window. The sun was rising.

She shook her head. In the dream she had seen two people fighting, but they were both herself. What did it mean?

The two wagons were in front of the house, packed and ready to go. Tsaluh saw why there was so little room for her own clothes. One wagon was loaded with barrels of food—corn meal, flour, and salt pork. She hated the taste of salt pork, but she knew it would keep a long time.

People had said the new land was far away, but Tsaluh had not realized what that meant. "How long will the trip take?" she asked her father.

He shook his head. "We don't know," he said. "Maybe eighty days." The other wagon was filled with clothing, blankets, mattresses, pots and pans from the kitchen, and a few pieces of furniture.

Father put one last box inside. "The newspaper," he said. He had saved all the copies of the Cherokee newspaper that was printed in the letters that Sequoyah had invented. "This must never be lost," he told Tsaluh. "Someday you will teach your own children to read."

Mother would drive one wagon, and Father

the other. The children and Grandmother could ride in back.

But Grandmother had gone back to her lodge. She said that she would stay, no matter what the others did.

"We can't leave her," Father said. "The soldiers will come and drive her off, and then she will be alone. She must come with us."

They took the wagons up the little dirt road that ran near Grandmother's lodge. As they approached, they could see smoke rising from the trees. "She's cooking breakfast," said Tsaluh.

But the smoke increased, and they saw that something larger than a cooking fire must be burning. Father jumped out of his wagon and rushed into the woods. Sarah and her brother Sam followed.

When they arrived, they saw Grandmother sitting on the ground with three soldiers around her. The soldiers had set her lodge on fire.

Grandmother was not hurt. Father helped her get up. "We'll take her with us," he told the soldiers, and they moved aside.

Grandmother let Father lead her away. She looked over her shoulder at the lodge and shrugged. "I'll come back and build another," she said.

Father shook his head. "We'll find a better place to live," he told her.

"We're going where the sun dies," Grandmother said. "The Dark Land. I will never live there."

Tsaluh took Grandmother's hand. It was cold. "Don't say that, Grandmother."

"I have seen the future," Grandmother said firmly.

Tsaluh shivered.

CHAPTER FOUR

Take My Spirit with You

TSALUH and her family drove their wagons to a big stockade that the soldiers had built. All the Cherokees had to assemble here so that they could travel west together.

Tsaluh saw how hard the trip was going to be. Some families, like hers, had brought enough things to begin a new life. But others had been driven out of their homes with little warning. They wrapped a few possessions in blankets and carried them on their backs.

The soldiers forced everyone into the stockades—mothers with newborn babies, sick people, old men and women who could barely walk. No one was allowed to stay behind.

In the rapid removal, families had already become separated. Some children had run into the woods when they saw the soldiers burning their homes. Husbands who had been out hunting found their families gone when they returned. People walked through the stockade asking if anyone had seen their loved ones.

Already, people were hungry. The soldiers ladled out bowls of porridge each morning and evening, but there was never enough of it. The Cherokees could easily have caught deer and rabbits, but they were not allowed to leave the stockade.

There was only one well for the whole camp. Twice a day, Tsaluh took a pail there to fill it for her family. It took her an hour each time, for hundreds of others waited in line for their turn to draw water.

Finally the day came to leave. A woman who was camped next to the Rogers had given birth to a child during the night. Mother and Grandmother had gone to help her. "It was a difficult birth," Mother said. "She should not walk, but they have no wagon."

Tsaluh looked at Sam, who nodded. "We can walk," they said. "Put her in our wagon." Gently, the woman's husband laid her on a blanket.

Tsaluh peeked over the side of the wagon. The woman looked up and smiled weakly.

"Can I see your baby?" Tsaluh asked. The woman opened the bundle that she held next to her heart. Sarah saw a frowning face with a shock of black hair. The baby began to cry.

Grandmother leaned over and whispered to Tsaluh. "He's hungry. Little mother hasn't got any milk for him yet. I gave them some herb tea."

The stockade gates opened, and the first wagons moved forward. A thousand people followed, some walking, some riding on horseback, some in wagons. The journey began. Those who lived through it would call it *nunna-da-ul-tsun-yi,* "the trail on which they wept."

Tsaluh was used to running in the fields all day. But she soon discovered that walking for hours next to a slow-moving wagon was tiring. As the sun rose higher in the sky, she grew thirsty. But she knew they had to be careful with the water. Whatever they could carry in the wagon had to last until they came to a stream. She swallowed hard, and forced herself to walk on without asking for something to drink.

When the sun went down, she wanted to

throw herself onto the ground and sleep. But they had to gather wood to make campfires. Everyone shared what little food they had. John Ross's brother Lewis had gone ahead to buy food at towns along the way. But often the meat was spoiled and the corn meal was filled with worms.

At night, men sneaked away from the camp to hunt game. Sometimes they brought back a deer, but usually they could catch only rabbits, squirrels, or raccoons. There was never enough for everyone to eat.

Day after day they went on. A week passed, then a month, two months. Tsaluh began to think they would walk forever. It began to rain, and the road turned into a sea of mud. Wagons got stuck, and the line stopped while people got out and pushed them onward.

The horses and oxen that pulled the Cherokees' wagons were tired too. Families began to discard some of their belongings to make the load lighter. Tsaluh's mother threw away the sewing table that had been a wedding present. Then Father's favorite chair. Finally the mattresses went too. The road behind was strewn with all the things that reminded them of their old home.

To Tsaluh, the soft mud was a relief, for her feet were always sore from the endless days of walking. But she soon found that it was more tiring to walk in the mud. Her feet sank up to the ankles and made a sucking sound when she pulled them out. Each step forward became an effort. Exhausted, she held on to the side of the wagon to help herself move on.

Many in the marching throng became ill. The harsh sounds of children coughing echoed through the camp at night. Some of those who lay down to sleep did not get up again. Almost every day now began with the digging of graves.

Tsaluh slept in the wagon with Grandmother and the woman with the baby. One morning Grandmother shook Tsaluh awake. "Unbutton your dress," Grandmother said. "Let me see your skin."

Grandmother examined her quickly. "You don't have them," she said.

"What are you looking for?" Tsaluh asked.

"Red spots," Grandmother said. "The woman had the red-spot sickness. She is dead."

Tsaluh glanced at the woman. Grandmother had already covered her face. "What about the baby?" Tsaluh said.

"He died yesterday, but she would not let him

go," said Grandmother. "We will bury them together."

The woman's husband stood silently as his
wife and child were lowered into the ground.
There was no time for a proper ceremony, just a
few words and a prayer. The living had to move
on. The man left behind his loved ones with
only a hastily carved piece of wood to mark their
resting place.

After a few days, Tsaluh did not see him walking with them anymore. She thought he might
have tried to sneak away and go back home.
But when people did this, the soldiers usually
caught and punished them.

The line of wagons moved north. The weather
grew colder. Some mornings the water barrels
had a crust of ice on top. So many more people
fell sick that every family with a wagon carried
some.

Tsaluh and Sam continued to walk. Grandmother made them moccasins out of tree bark.
Tsaluh was glad Mother had made her bring a
coat, but many people had nothing but thin
blankets to wrap around themselves.

All the spare food had been eaten, and they
lived on whatever they could find along the way.
Tsaluh was always hungry. She kept thinking of

the days when Mother baked bread at home, and the smell filled the whole house. Her mouth watered.

The line of Cherokees reached the Ohio River. Ferryboats took them across, but it took two days for everyone to reach the other side. Tsaluh heard that the ferry captains charged them twice as much as they usually did.

While they waited, Tsaluh climbed into the wagon. It was good to have a day to rest. She saw that Grandmother was still knitting the strands for Tsaluh's medicine belt.

Grandmother took some herbs and roots from her own belt. She started to explain what each was, and how it could be used. "So many things to tell you," she said. "I thought I had more time."

"Grandmother," said Tsaluh. "The night before we left home I had a dream. I didn't understand what it meant."

"Tell me," Grandmother said.

Tsaluh explained about seeing Sarah and Tsaluh fighting on the bank of the river. "But now we're here at the river, and nothing has happened."

"This is not the great river," said Grandmother. "Another one, much bigger, lies ahead of us. Then you will fight. I will help you. You will get across. But I will not."

"Don't say that, Grandmother. You have to teach me more. I can't learn how to use the medicines unless you come with us."

Grandmother shook her head. "You will take my spirit with you. But I will never go where the sun dies." She pressed her finger against Tsaluh's mouth. "Don't argue. I have already seen the Raven Mockers. I chased them away, but they will return."

Tsaluh's eyes filled with tears. "I need you, Grandmother," she said.

Grandmother wrapped the belt around Tsaluh's waist. "Not finished yet," she said. "Listen to me. I have seen something else. When you reach the other side, and you have questions, someone will come to answer them for you."

"Who?"

"You'll know when you see him."

The Cherokees crossed the river and moved on. Winter winds blew here, colder than any that ever blew in the land of the Cherokees. Tsaluh lowered her head against the icy blasts and walked on. They had been traveling for more than eighty days.

At last they reached the great river, the Mississippi. It was wider than any Tsaluh had ever seen. And worse, it was filled with chunks of ice. No boats could travel across it now. They would have to wait.

The people of the nearby town would not shelter the Cherokees in their houses. The *unaka* townsfolk were afraid of them, for they had been told the Cherokees were fierce Indians, ready to kill and steal.

The soldiers promised that supplies would soon arrive, but none came. The Cherokees had to hunt for their own food. They had nothing but blankets to make shelters against the cold. They searched the barren land for firewood to warm themselves.

And there, day after day, more of them died. Tsaluh went from wagon to wagon, bringing herb tea that Grandmother brewed. She took crying babies in her arms, trying to comfort those whose mothers lay ill. Sam brought wood to keep the fire at their camp burning.

Tsaluh walked down to the river and looked across. A white mist covered the land on the other side. The ice still choked the brown water. And now it began to snow.

She brushed the flakes off her face. Something was wrong. She wasn't cold any longer. Her head was warm. She felt dizzy. She barely managed to stagger back to the wagon.

Hands lifted her inside. "I'll take care of her," she heard Grandmother say. "She'll be all right."

Grandmother covered her with a blanket, but it was too hot and Tsaluh tried to kick it off. "Lie still," Grandmother said. "The Raven Mockers are all around us."

Grandmother opened Tsaluh's dress and put herbs and grasses onto her chest. She pressed a leaf inside Tsaluh's mouth. It tasted bitter. "Suck on it," Grandmother said.

Tsaluh fell asleep. Her dream came to her again. Tsaluh and Sarah were fighting. She twisted her body, trying to free her arms from the blanket. Someone held her close. "Don't worry," she heard Grandmother say. "I'm still here."

Tsaluh opened her eyes. Grandmother's face was next to hers. Grandmother set a twig on fire and blew the smoke into Tsaluh's face. It smelled sweet. "Breathe in," Grandmother said.

She slept again, but this time without a dream. Sometimes she heard Grandmother's voice, chanting the old, old Cherokee songs that she had learned from her own mother long ago.

Tsaluh tried to listen, so she would remember, but she drifted back into sleep.

When she awoke, the sun was shining. She felt much better. She lifted the blanket and found that Grandmother had finished the medicine belt and tied it around her waist. The pouch on it was full. Tsaluh opened it and found that Grandmother had put all her medicines inside it.

But where was Grandmother? Tsaluh sat up and listened. People were singing. A lot of people together. She looked over the side of the wagon. A crowd of Cherokees had gathered at the edge of the camp. Tsaluh got down from the wagon and walked toward them.

Some of the people turned when she came up and moved aside to let her through. Someone had died and was being buried. She saw her mother and father and Sam standing by the edge of the grave. But where was Grandmother?

When Tsaluh's mother looked at her, Tsaluh knew. She forced herself to take the last few steps forward. Grandmother lay there, her arms folded and her eyes closed. Her face was peaceful. Tsaluh fell to her knees and felt the tears flow down her cheeks.

Mother put her arms around Tsaluh. "She just

went to sleep and did not wake up," Mother whispered. "She did not want to cross the river."

"I know," Tsaluh said. She looked up to the sky. The sun was shining brightly for the first time in days. "She wanted to stay here, in the land of the sun."

CHAPTER FIVE

Another Teacher

THE SUN melted the ice in the river, and the wagons lined up to cross. As the boat carried the Rogers family over, Tsaluh looked back at the spot where Grandmother lay under the earth. I will carry your spirit, she promised. I will remember everything that happened. And I will never forgive the *unakas* for what they have done.

The journey was still not over. The snow fell heavily now, and people's feet froze walking the long, long trail. More rivers had to be crossed, more hunger had to be endured, more disease, and more deaths.

By the time they reached their new land, almost one out of every four Cherokees had died on the trail. Tsaluh's group took 115 days to make the journey. The journey for other groups was even longer.

While winter lasted, they stayed at Fort Gibson, which the soldiers had built on the edge of the new Cherokee lands. The government, as it had promised, gave them land, horses, cows, and food. But nothing that the Cherokees received was as good as what they had left behind.

The land set aside as "Indian territory" was empty because no one wanted it. The cattle they were given were so thin they could hardly stand. The food was so poor that it only made more people sick.

But the Cherokees started over. They strung their bows and hunted deer and squirrels. They cut down trees and burned the stumps to make room for cotton and corn. Sometimes their plows broke in the hard soil. The seedlings withered when the rain did not come on time. The Cherokees planted again and dug ditches to bring water from the muddy streams.

Tsaluh worked harder than she ever had in her life. She carried stones to build the foundation of their new house. She made blankets on a loom and pots to replace the ones they had lost.

She learned how to skin a deer and dry the hide in the sun for clothing.

All of the old skills of the Cherokees were needed now, and those who remembered taught them to others. One of the first things the Cherokees did was to build a school where their young people could learn. They began to print their newspaper again, using both Cherokee and English.

But Tsaluh would not read the English words when the teacher called on her. She shook her head and said she hated the *unakas'* language.

All her family except Grandmother had always called her Sarah. Now she would answer only if they used her real name, Tsaluh.

One day John Ross came to visit. He looked weary and sad. His wife had died on the journey west. People said she had given her blanket to a sick child, and the cold rain had given her a chill.

Tsaluh looked at him sitting in their house. She saw only a man dressed in the suit and tie that the *unakas* wore. John Ross always wore those clothes. Tsaluh hated them because they reminded her of what the *unakas* had done. She turned and left the house.

She ran into the tall grass that grew on the hill

behind their house. She threw herself down and began to cry.

It was very rude to treat a guest this way. But the Cherokees did not punish their children. They expected them to learn by watching what the adults did. If a child did something wrong, she would have to find it out for herself.

Tsaluh knew she had been rude. If she had been at home, she would have walked up the hill to Grandmother's lodge. Grandmother would always listen to her and tell her what she wanted to know.

"Grandmother, Grandmother," Tsaluh sobbed. "Why did you have to die? I need you."

She heard a whispering sound in the grass and looked up, thinking it might be a snake.

A man stood looking down at her. He had a cloth wrapped around his head, like the older Cherokees wore. He carried a long walking stick, and she saw that one of his legs was shorter than the other.

"Are you all right?" he asked Tsaluh.

She wiped the tears from her eyes and nodded.

"I wonder if you can help me," he said. "I heard that the Rogers family is living around here."

"That's my family," she replied. "Our house is down at the bottom of the hill."

"I came to see if a woman named Kituwha lived with them."

Tsaluh was surprised. "Kituwha was my grandmother's name. But she . . . she died on the trail when we left our land."

"I am sorry," he said softly. "I hoped to see her once more."

"Did you know her?" Tsaluh asked.

"Long ago," he said. "She was a beautiful young woman." He looked at her. "I can see her face in yours. Yes. It is nearly the same."

Tsaluh had never thought what Grandmother must have been like when she was young.

"She was a *ghighau* of our people," Tsaluh explained. "She helped me to fight Sarah when I was sick. And then she died." She felt the tears flow down her cheeks again.

The man sat down slowly because his leg bothered him. Tsaluh could see his face more clearly. He was old, but his eyes were full of life. "That seems strange," he said.

"No, it's true," Tsaluh said. "Look." She opened the pouch that Grandmother had put around her waist. "She gave me her medicines."

He examined the herbs and roots in the

pouch, naming each one as he touched it. "Yes, these are all good medicines. Kituwha must have learned how to use them from her own mother, who was also a *ghighau*. That does not surprise me. But who is this Sarah who brought the sickness?"

Tsaluh hung her head. "It was me. That is my *unaka* name." She told him about her dream. "Grandmother said that when we came to the river, she would help me fight. But when I awoke from my illness, she had died. And now I hate all the *unakas* because they killed her."

The man sat looking out across the valley. For a long time he did not speak. Then he said, "I think you did not understand what your dream meant."

Tsaluh thought about this. "Grandmother said I would find someone else on this side of the river who would answer my questions."

He nodded. "I heard you asking a question before, when I walked up the hill."

Tsaluh remembered. "I asked Grandmother why she had to die."

"That is an easy question. Because everyone has to die. But you know that those who die on Earth go to live among the stars. We think they are happier there. And someday we will join

them." He smiled at her and said, "You are old enough to know what we Cherokees do a year after a person has died."

Tsaluh nodded. "We make a big meal for her, and then when all her friends and family eat it, we tell the dead person how much we loved her."

"And so you will do that, for you loved your grandmother."

"But she is not here," Tsaluh said. "Her body lies at the edge of the big river. She would not cross it."

"Why not?"

"Because the sun does not shine here."

He smiled and pointed to the sky. "But you see it does."

Tsaluh blinked. Of course it did.

"So," the old man said, "when your grandmother learns that, her spirit will come here."

"I promised to carry her spirit wherever I went."

"So you have. And your grandmother did not die fighting Sarah, because she would have been fighting you. Your grandmother fought the sickness that you had."

"But then why were Tsaluh and Sarah fighting in my dream?"

The old man pulled at his ear, thinking. "You were troubled because you had to leave your home. You may have thought Sarah caused that trouble. But it is not good to fight yourself."

He touched a bright yellow flower growing in the grass next to him. "What is this?" he asked.

"A flower," Tsaluh said, "but I don't know its name."

"People here call it a coneflower. But perhaps that is not its real name. Maybe the flower has a secret name for itself, that people do not know."

His deep brown eyes peered into hers. "What would that name be?"

"I don't know," she said.

He nodded. "The flower does not speak, but we do. So we give it a name. Names are powerful. That was why your grandmother wanted you to be Tsaluh—so that you would be Cherokee. But what if we gave the flower another name? Would that change the flower?"

"No, it would be the same flower," said Tsaluh.

He spread his hands and smiled. "You see that is true. So really, Sarah and Tsaluh should not fight at all. They are the same person."

"But Sarah is an *unaka* name. And I hate the *unakas* because of what they have done to us."

The man waved his hand at her. "That is the way Andrew Jackson thought. He did not understand that Cherokees are people just the same as him. So he wanted to push us away from his people. But that was foolish."

He pointed to another flower growing nearby, a blue one. "Is this a flower too?"

"Yes," she said.

"But it grows in the same place as the yellow one. Someday, that will happen with people too."

He gestured toward the prairie that stretched into the distance. It was covered with flowers of all kinds. "See them. They grow well because the sun here is bright and the land is good. Be Tsaluh. Be Sarah. You will grow strong and blossom too. And so will all the Cherokees."

He looked around for his walking stick, and began to get up.

"What is *your* name?" Tsaluh asked.

"I too have more than one name. Some people call me George Guess. But I am also known as Sequoyah."

"Sequoyah?" She jumped up and helped him to his feet. "You are the one who thought up a way to write our language?"

"Yes, I did that."

"I can read anything in Cherokee," she said proudly. "Come down to our house and I'll show you."

"I would be honored," he said.

"And will you tell me how to use all the medicines Grandmother gave me?"

"I will try."

"And maybe you will stay long enough to share the meal we will have for Grandmother next year?"

"We'll see, we'll see."

Sequoyah did not stay with the Rogers family that long. He was, as Grandmother had told Tsaluh, a wanderer. He headed farther west. "The world is big," he told Tsaluh. "I want to see as much of it as I can." He never returned.

But when the Rogers family made the meal for Grandmother's spirit, Tsaluh felt that Sequoyah's spirit was there too. She stood up to speak. "Grandmother, I met the teacher you said I would find. I know that you guided him here. He finished teaching me what you did not have time for. Thank you for saving me. However long I live, I promise to hold your spirit always in my heart." And she did until the day when she joined Grandmother in the stars.

MAKING A
MEDICINE BELT

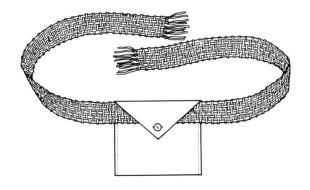

NATIVE Americans used all kinds of materials to make cloth. They wove thin strips of tree bark, vines, grass, and other plants, as well as feathers, porcupine quills, and the fur of animals. They colored their cloth with dyes made from berries, bark, roots, leaves, and flower petals. You can use any kind of yarn you choose to make a belt.

To weave blankets and other large pieces of cloth, Native Americans used a loom. Small belts, bracelets, and headbands could be woven on sticks and even on the fingers. The method described below uses drinking straws in place of sticks.

Materials Needed

(for belt)
Ball of yarn, Five paper or plastic drinking straws, Scissors, Paper punch.

(for medicine pouch)
Needle and thread, Button, Piece of cloth about four inches by ten inches.

Steps

1. Start by winding a piece of yarn around your waist three times. You will need the extra length. Make five strands of yarn the same length.
2. Pinch flat one end of each of the five straws. Punch a hole in each of the five flat ends.
3. Thread one of the strands of yarn through each hole. Pull the yarn through so that both ends are together. The yarn you weave will be pushed down onto these hanging strands.
4. Lie the five straws together in a row. Take the rest of your yarn and tie one end to the bottom straw. Put your knot near the punched end.
5. Start weaving by winding the yarn over and

under each straw. When you reach the top straw, turn the yarn around it and weave back down, going under and over. Continue going up and down until you have several inches of weaving.
6. Slide the weaving off the straws onto the hanging strands. Keep weaving more yarn in the same way, sliding it down the strands as you go. Save about three inches of the strands at each end.

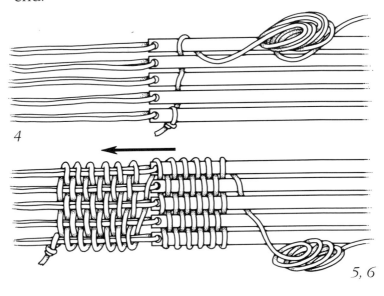

4

5, 6

7. When you have finished weaving, tie the last end around the top straw before you slide it off.
8. Now tie knots in each hanging strand at both ends of the belt. These will keep the belt from unraveling.

Tips

You can experiment with different colors of yarn to make a pattern in the belt. Tie each end of each piece of yarn when you start and stop.

You can make a medicine pouch for the belt by cutting a piece of cloth or leather in a shape like this:

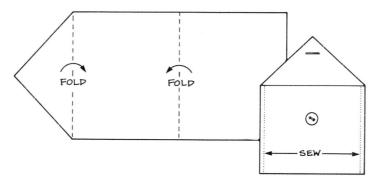

Fold the cloth up and sew along the sides. Cut and sew a button hole in the flap. Sew a button onto the top of the pouch to close it.

ADDITIONAL TITLES AVAILABLE
IN THE **HER STORY** SERIES,

by Dorothy and Thomas Hoobler:

Read the story of . . .

Sarah Tsaluh Rogers in
The Trail on Which They Wept:
The Story of a Cherokee Girl
By Hoobler & Hoobler/Burrus
LSB 0-382-24331-5
jh/c 0-382-24333-1
s/c 0-382-24353-6

Amy Elizabeth Harris in
Treasure in the Stream:
The Story of a Gold Rush Girl
By Hoobler & Hoobler/Carpenter
LSB 0-382-24144-4
jh/c 0-382-24151-7
s/c 0-382-24346-3

Maria Hernandez in
A Promise at the Alamo:
The Story of a Texas Girl
By Hoobler & Hoobler/Hewitson
LSB 0-382-24147-9
jh/c 0-382-24154-1
s/c 0-382-24352-8

Annie Laurie MacDougal in
The Sign Painter's Secret:
The Story of a Revolutionary Girl
By Hoobler & Hoobler/Ayers
LSB 0-382-24143-6
jh/c 0-382-24150-9
s/c 0-382-24345-5

Fran Parker in
And Now,
a Word from our Sponsor:
The Story of a Roaring '20's Girl
By Hoobler & Hoobler/Leer
LSB 0-382-24146-0
jh/c 0-382-24153-3
s/c 0-382-24350-1

Emily in
Next Stop, Freedom:
The Story of a Slave Girl
By Hoobler & Hoobler/Hanna
LSB 0-382-24145-2
jh/c 0-382-24152-5
s/c 0-382-24347-1

Laura Ann Barnes in
Aloha Means Come Back:
The Story of a World War II Girl
By Hoobler & Hoobler/Bleck
LSB 0-382-24148-7
jh/c 0-382-24156-8
s/c 0-382-24349-8

Christina Ricci in
Summer of Dreams:
The Story of a World's Fair Girl
By Hoobler & Hoobler/Graef
LSB 0-382-24332-3
jh/c 0-382-24335-8
s/c 0-382-24354-4

"This is a well-written and informative series with believable characters."
— American Bookseller "Pick of the Lists"

For price information or to place an order, call toll-free 1-800-848-9500.